PENELOPE
TERROR IN THE
HARBOUR
SHARON E. MCKAY

Penguin Books

PENGUIN BOOKS
Published by the Penguin Group

Penguin Books Canada Ltd, 10 Alcorn Avenue, Toronto, Ontario,
Canada M4V 3B2

Penguin Books Ltd, 27 Wrights Lane, London W8 5TZ, England

Penguin Putnam Inc., 375 Hudson Street, New York, New York 10014, U.S.A

Penguin Books Australia Ltd, Ringwood, Victoria, Australia

Penguin Books (NZ) Ltd, cnr Rosedale and Airborne Roads, Albany,
Auckland 1310, New Zealand

Penguin Books Ltd, Registered Offices: Harmondsworth, Middlesex, England

DESIGN: MATTHEWS COMMUNICATIONS DESIGN INC.

MAP ILLUSTRATION: SHARON MATTHEWS

INTERIOR ILLUSTRATIONS: RON LIGHTBURN

First published, 2001

3   5   7   9   10   8   6   4

Manufactured in Canada

NATIONAL LIBRARY OF CANADA CATALOGUING IN PUBLICATION DATA

McKay, Sharon E.

Terror in the harbour : Penelope

(Our Canadian girl)

ISBN 0-14-100329-4

1. Halifax (N.S.)—History—Explosion, 1917—Juvenile fiction.
I. Title. II. Series.

PS8575.K2898T47 2001   jC813'.6 C2001-901161-X

PZ7.M192Te 2001

Visit Penguin Canada's website at **www.penguin.ca**

PENELOPE
TERROR IN THE
HARBOUR
SHARON E. MCKAY

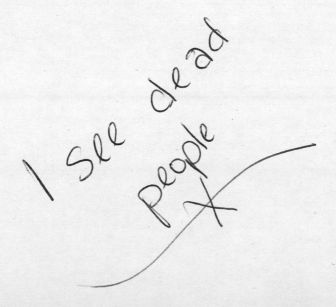

I see dead people X

To Nichole,
the best
of big sisters

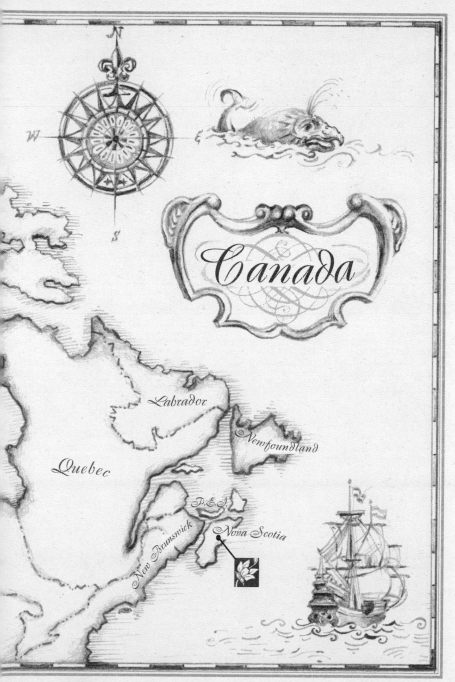

Canada

Labrador

Newfoundland

Quebec

P.E.I.

New Brunswick

Nova Scotia

 Marks the location of the story

MEET PENNY

THIS IS THE STORY OF PENNY, THE ELDEST DAUGHTER in a family of three girls. Penny's mother died a year ago. Now, Penny cares for her two little sisters while keeping up with her schoolwork. Penny's father is very serious about schoolwork, although most people think that women don't need much education to have babies and keep house.

It's 1917, and the Great War in Europe has been going on for three long years. Halifax is bursting at the seams with soldiers going to, and coming from, the war. Penny is often down at the docks, as her father has his office there. She has watched young, eager soldiers board the ships that will take them across the Atlantic. But Penny has also seen badly wounded men coming off the ships. Some with no arms, no legs; many leave the ships on stretchers; all look sad and broken.

It's not only the soldiers in Europe that must defend

Canada. Penny's teacher says that the people of Halifax must be on their guard too. German submarines lurk beneath the frigid waters of the Atlantic Ocean. Their intent is to torpedo ships carrying supplies and soldiers.

This morning, Penny has other things on her mind, mostly getting her little sisters over to the neighbour's house and not getting in trouble at school for being late, again! But something terrible will happen this day, something so horrifying, that Penny's life, and the lives of those around her, will be changed in the blink of an eye.

CHAPTER N°1

Penny pulled her nightcap down over her ears, the quilt up to her chin, and burrowed deep under the blankets. Except for Emily's murmuring on the other side of the bed, and Maggie's squeaky baby sounds from her cradle, all was quiet.

The sun would be up soon. The curtains would have to be pulled back if the morning light was to fill the room. But it was so cold! Penny dithered, counted to three, crawled over Emily, leapt out of bed, sped across the room, and

1

flung back the curtains. Hopping from one foot to the other, she pressed her nose against the frosty glass. It was black as pitch outside. The cobbled stones of Macara Street shimmered beneath the beam of a street light. It was December 6, and it still hadn't snowed. Two soldiers on horseback clomped on by. Soldiers were a common enough sight, since Wellington Barracks was just down the road. "They must be cold too," Penny thought, as she hurled herself back into bed and plunged under the covers to wait for daylight.

The back door downstairs squeaked. Papa was up and about. Penny could hear him fill up the scuttle with coal and toss it into the kitchen stove. Then the kettle landed on the stovetop with a thud. Now, Penny thought, Papa would wind Mama's clock, which stood on the mantel over the fire. Papa gave the clock three sharp grinds. Right on time! Penny giggled. You could know a lot about the world, if you were very still, if you listened hard enough.

It didn't take long for the heat from the stove to rise up and warm the bedroom. Penny loved their bedroom but the kitchen was the nicest room in the house, and their house was the nicest house in Halifax, no, in the world! She had helped Mama paint and wall paper the kitchen and the parlour too. They had made it a warm, welcoming home.

Papa had never liked it when Mama did heavy work. Said it wasn't fitting, her being a lady and all. "A lady?" Mama had teased him. "Since when has moving a paintbrush back and forth been considered heavy work?" She used to say that she was the happiest person in Halifax, and if he kept on at her, he would only make her miserable. Then he'd laugh too. Sometimes he'd swing Mama around the kitchen and her long blond hair would unravel from the bun at the back of her head and fall onto her shoulders. Emily had been littler then, like Maggie was now. Back then, Maggie had just been a lump in Mama's tummy.

A lady. Penny thought on that. Mama had come from an important family in Halifax. Mama's papa had been rich, but he was dead now. Mama's own mother, Penny's grandmother, was still alive, although she had moved to a grand house in Montreal just after Mama married Papa. Penny was named after her Grandmother Penelope. She shuddered. It was a silly, old-fashioned name. What she wouldn't give to be called Lily or May. Besides, Grandma Penelope had never even acknowledged her existence.

Papa's family lived across the sea in Ireland, all except his sister in Toronto. The only family Penny really knew was Aunt Colleen, Mama's cousin. Aunt Colleen had a brother named Robert. He drove a great big automobile. He said that she should call him Robert, not Uncle Robert. He said uncles were all old, stodgy fellows with moustaches. He was young and far too good-looking. He made her laugh. But it was Aunt Colleen she remembered most. Penny whispered the name in the dark. *Collll-eeeee-nnnn*. It rolled off her tongue just right. After Mama had married Papa, no one from Mama's family would talk to her, no one except Aunt Colleen and Robert. Then Aunt Colleen had moved to Montreal to live with Grandmother Penelope.

Penny heard Papa open a cupboard door, close it again and take the kettle off the stove. He'd be making himself a mug of tea before he left for work. Papa worked hard. He had to, he said. Halifax was booming what with all the war work. Papa had his own business. He was an (Penelope paused to think of the words) independent contractor. That was right. He built the insides of buildings, the innards he said. He always laughed when he said that. But Papa didn't laugh so much now, not since Mama died.

Tips of morning light began to push back the night sky. Soon Papa would be out the door and she'd not see him again until nightfall. Then she had an idea. If she hurried she could make Papa breakfast. Penny flipped back the covers and swung her legs over the side of the bed. Emily grunted and curled up like a cooked shrimp. While one hand reached for her robe, Penny's toes searched the floor very carefully for her slippers. Emily was only five years old and didn't always push the po back under the bed.

"Penny, where are you going?" Emily mumbled from the other side of the bed.

"Don't wake up," Penny whispered, "it's too early."

"I'm cold," she murmured.

"Hush, now. You'll wake the baby. Go back to sleep."

Penny cast an eye over to Maggie's cradle. Her fat little feet were already touching the end. It was time she went into a proper crib. Maggie's first birthday wasn't far off. But how would they be able to celebrate knowing that it was the same day Mama died?

With her robe tied firmly around her, Penny yanked off her bed cap and looped an old, frayed ribbon around her long hair. Almost instantly strands of hair came loose. "Oh drat," she sighed in frustration. She hated her hair. It never did what she wanted it to do. It was long, almost to her waist, and it was red! "Auburn," Papa called it. "Beautiful Irish hair." It didn't seem fair that both Maggie and Emily had Mama's soft blond hair, and Mama's pretty looks, too.

There was nothing Penny liked about her looks. Mrs. Hanson, the lady who lived two doors down and cared for Maggie and Emily while Penny went to school, said that she was "a long drink of water." Then she'd say to anyone who'd listen, "And would ya' look at the child's colouring! A ghost has more to say for itself."

It was true, she was skinny, bony like a bicycle, all knobs and spokes. And, to top it off, she had green eyes! "Irish eyes," Papa said. Ireland, Penny grumbled, had to be filled with funny-looking girls.

Penny crept out of the bedroom, padded down the stairs and walked into the kitchen.

"Morning, Papa."

"Sure, darlin', it's too early. Back to bed with you." Papa spoke kindly. His smile went all the way up to his eyes.

"But I want to make you some breakfast." Penny reached into the larder and pulled out a basket of eggs.

Mrs. Hanson was always saying, "That man is too thin. He needs fattening up."

"I've made the porridge, that will do me right," Papa insisted.

Mama's clock struck the quarter hour.

Even if she couldn't make him breakfast Penny didn't want to go back to bed. She hardly ever had Papa to herself. Then she saw it.

"What's that?" Penny pointed to a large, brown box on the kitchen table.

"I was just about to put that away but..." Papa dithered. He pushed back a shock of salt-and-pepper hair and grinned. "No reason why you can't have it now."

"For me?" Penny all but threw herself on the box. It wasn't even her birthday, and Christmas was weeks away!

"Easy now." He smiled again as he picked up his tea and eased himself into the rocking chair by the stove.

Penny tore off the top of the box and peered inside. Carefully, as carefully as if she were unwrapping the finest china, Penny folded back the tissue paper. Her breath all but left her.

"Papa!" This was too much! Too expensive. Too pretty. Too everything!

"It's time you had a proper dress. Your mother would have wanted you to have it," said Papa, his voice barely above a whisper.

"But a store-bought dress!" Penny lifted the dress out of the box and held it against her. It was blue, the colour of Mama's eyes, and belted just below the waist, with a bit of lace at the throat. It was a lady's dress.

"There's more." Papa pointed to the box.

"Underthings and all. The saleslady said you'd be needing them." For reasons Penny didn't quite understand, Papa turned pink.

Penny peered back into the box and touched the petticoat.

"You'll be needing a hat, and shoes, but those will have to be fitted proper," said Papa as he took a sip of his tea.

A thought started to creep into her mind. What was it for? Why would she be needing a store-bought dress? She had two dresses as it was, and a dress for church. That was more than most girls her age had. And then she knew, and the knowledge made her knees tremble. Penny pitched the dress back in the box.

"What's wrong? Don't you like it?" Papa asked, his voice rising.

Penny spun around. It was all she could do not to shout.

"What's it for?" Her eyes brimmed with tears.

"Oh, Penny." Papa leaned back into the rocker. With a long, slow breath he said, "I've received a

Penny lifted the dress out of the box and held it against her. It was blue, the colour of Mama's eyes. It was a lady's dress.

letter from your grandmother."

That's it! She was right. He meant to send her away. He meant her to go and live with Grandmother Penelope in Montreal. Tears bubbled up and slid down her face. Her lips quivered.

"I won't go!" The words spilled out of her with such force that she stumbled forward and gripped the edge of the table. "Why? Why do you want me to go?"

"Come here, love." Papa held out his arms.

"No! You don't love me." Her words hung in the air like laundry on the line, going nowhere, just hanging.

"Penny."

"No. No." Penny thumped down onto a kitchen chair and covered her face with her hands.

"Ach, darlin', hear me out," Papa said softly. "You're a beautiful wee girl. A father never had a more lovely daughter. And I love ya' more than life itself. But you have so much ahead of you, school, maybe university. Your mother and I talked about our daughters going to the university. Sure, can ya' think on that, what it would mean for a man like myself to have educated daughters? But here, livin' like this . . ."

"Like what?" Penny interrupted. "Mama loved this house. It's a fine house."

Penny looked past her father and caught the edge of a roll of blueprints that were on top of the kitchen cupboards. They were for the house Papa had been going to build for Mama. It would have been the most beautiful house in Halifax, Papa said so. If only Mama hadn't died and Maggie hadn't been born. Tears spilled down Penny's face.

"Penny, listen to me." Papa braced himself as though he was trying to steel himself against a north wind. "You're doing work meant for a grown woman, taking care of babies, running a house. It's not right. You should be living with someone who can tell you what a young girl needs to know, about woman things. And now, with your grandmother's letter…" Papa ran his hands through his hair. "Your Aunt Colleen is in Montreal. You like her, don't you? Sure, your own mother loved her dearly. And your grandmother says that you'll go to a good girls' school. You'll be raised like a lady. You'll meet fine people in Montreal."

"What about Maggie and Emily? Who will take care of them?" Penny glared at her father with marble-hard eyes.

"Mrs. Hanson will, same as she does now. Business is good," Papa carried on. "Soon I'll be able to afford help full time. Someone to come in like, and take care of the house too."

"You'll get married again. That's what Mrs. Hanson says. She says that Margie Flynn has her cap set on you." Penny's words came out in sputters.

Papa laughed. To Penny it felt like a slap in the face.

"Oh my love, is that what you think? That I'm getting rid of you to marry someone?" Papa stopped laughing and looked at her steadily. "Come here."

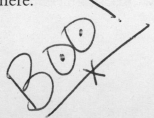

Slowly she walked over to her father and crumpled into his lap. He rocked her back and forth, as though she were a baby and not all of ten years old.

"When your mother came into my life I thought that I'd been kissed by an angel. She was the most beautiful woman I had ever seen."

Penny nodded. Mama used to tell the story as though it were a fairytale. She'd make it sound as though she'd been a prisoner princess locked up in a castle, and only Papa's love had set her free.

"There I was, a man just starting out, an Irishman at that. I was doing work on a grand house. Most grand folks don't take too kindly to the Irish."

Penny nodded again. It was true. Even in the street they lived on, she heard people say "the dirty Irish." Why? Papa wasn't dirty.

"Poor folk and posh folk don't mix, you know that. And all I had to offer her was my heart. But it was enough. She was as kind and as good as she was lovely," Papa whispered. "Penny darlin', if I have one wish for my girls it's that you three find the love your mother and I had. Marry again? Where on God's earth would I find someone who could hold a candle to her?"

It was then that Penny realized how lonely he must be.

"Papa, I miss her too."

"I know you do, my darlin'. But she's here. I know that she's lookin' out for us." Papa gave her a hug just as Mama's clock struck five. "There now, the men will be waiting on me. Sure, it wouldn't do for the boss to come in late, now would it?" Papa kissed the top of Penny's head and eased her up onto her feet. "You go to your bed now. Run along."

Penny struggled to stand up. She was bone-weary, as though the day had already been spent.

Papa put on his winter jacket, wrapped a muffler around his throat and pulled on his gloves. "We'll talk more tonight, all right?"

There was nothing Penny could do but nod.

Papa opened the door and was gone.

She ran her hand over the soft wool dress. Just think, Papa had picked it out just for her. It wasn't the dress's fault that she had to go away. But nothing was settled, not yet.

Penny gathered up the box and climbed the stairs. She hung the dress on the outside of the wardrobe so that she could see it from her bed.

Light streamed up over the horizon. If she strained she could look out the window and see the sun rising over the Eastern Passage. There was mist in the harbour but that would soon fade away. It would be a beautiful day. Penny covered Maggie's fat feet with the blanket and, slipping off her robe and slippers, crawled back into bed. She put her arm around Emily and pulled the sleeping child in close. Her little body was warm and comforting.

"I love you, Emily. I don't want to leave you. I don't want to leave this house."

Sleep came unbidden.

CHAPTER 2

"Penny. PEN-EEEEEEY!"

Billy, Mrs. Hanson's boy, stood outside on the cobblestone road and yelled up at Penny's bedroom window.

"PEN-EEEEEE. GET UP!"

Penny bolted up in bed.

"PEN-EEEEEE!" Billy yelled for the third time.

The time! What time was it?

"Penny, what's wrong?" Emily murmured, just as baby Maggie let out a wail.

"PEN-EEEEEE!"

Billy Hanson, the most spoiled boy in the world, on account of his being the only boy in a household of five sisters, stood in his best winter coat and Buster Brown suit (and it wasn't even Sunday) and kept yelling his fool head off.

"Put your slippers on," said Penny to Emily as she leapt out of bed. "Billy," she yelled towards the window. "Hold on." And then, plop!

"Ohhh," Penny moaned, "the po!"

Its contents splattered all over the floor as the pot spun across the room.

"Ohhh," Penny moaned again. "Oh no."

"Penny, you spilled the piss-pot!" Emily sat up and giggled.

"The what? Who taught you that?" Penny scowled. But she knew, she absolutely knew! "It was Billy Hanson, wasn't it?" She shook with indignation as Emily's bottom lip quivered. "It's a very rude word, Emily. What would Papa say? What would Mama say?"

"I'm sorry, Penny." Emily sniffed as she rubbed her eyes with two balled-up fists.

"Sorry isn't good enough."

"PEN-EEEEEEE!"

"Stop it!" Penny leapt over the mess, flung open the window and stared down at Billy Hanson's miserable, good-for-nothing face. "Billy Hanson, if you don't stop yelling this minute I am going to give you your own head in your hands to play with." If she could have reached him, Penny would have throttled him right on the spot.

"Mama says that you are going to be late for school," Billy called back in a most self-satisfied way.

Penny leaned out the window and saw all the Hanson sisters walking down the street towards school. How? How could she have overslept?

"Tell her that I will have Maggie and Emily there as fast as I can." Penny slammed the window shut.

"Penny, Maggie's nappy smells bad." As if on cue, Maggie kicked off her blanket and let out a wail.

"She will have to wait." Penny flung Emily a pair of stockings and knickers. "Put them on, and hurry!"

Using the water from the water jug, and towels far too good for the purpose, Penny set to work cleaning the floor. She'd have to give it a real scrub when she got back from school.

Penny then pulled on her own stockings, knickers, woollen chest protector, wool skirt, blouse, and sweater.

"Pen-eee, I'm cold." Emily stomped her feet.

"Here." Penny braided her hair into one fat plait and tossed Emily the rest of her clothes. "Take them down to the kitchen and dress in front of the stove." Her heart sank. The kitchen fire would be out by now.

Penny heaved Maggie up onto her hip and almost gagged. How could a baby smell this bad?

She grabbed a nappy and new clothes for the baby, and thought about school. She'd miss morning prayers, the second time this month.

"Emily, put your slippers on. Come on."

With Maggie fussing and struggling in her arms, Penny thumped down the stairs, charged into the kitchen and plunked Maggie down in her chair. She peered into the stove. One red ember stood out from all the other crusty, grey coals. A little paper and kindling and she'd have it going again.

It took hardly any time to get Maggie put right, and set the kettle to boil, and reheat the porridge that Papa had left in the saucepan, and button up Emily's dress and jumper. There was nothing she couldn't handle, nothing she couldn't do.

Penny spooned the porridge into two bowls and plopped one in front of Emily. "Eat!" She glared at the five-year-old before turning to the baby. "Come on, Maggie, open wide." A spoonful of glob missed Maggie's mouth entirely and dangled from her chin. "Oh Maggie, please be a good girl." Penny jammed another spoonful of porridge into Maggie's mouth.

The back door opened and in fell Billy Hanson.

"Did ya' see it?" He was breathless, but nine-year-old irritating boys often are.

"You taught Emily a rude word. Go away." Penny fed Maggie another spoonful.

"What word?" Billy asked. There had been many.

"I'm not repeating it. Come on, Maggie, open up," Penny pleaded.

"Piss-pot!" said Emily. She was just trying to help, really she was.

"Emily!" This was all too much.

"Never mind that. Come and see the smoke!" Mud from Billy's feet flew in all directions. "Down at the harbour. Maybe ten ships crashed! Maybe twenty!" He was positively beaming. Nothing like a disaster to make a small boy happy.

"Don't be silly. And look at your shoes!" Penny glared down at the floor, then up at the clock. It was almost nine! Mr. Shirley was the meanest teacher in Halifax. She'd be in some trouble now.

Billy picked up one foot, then the other, and examined each with interest. Yep, there was mud on his shoes all right.

"Billy Hanson, look at the mess you are making. Get out! You are the silliest boy in Halifax, and shouldn't you be in school?" Another glob of porridge went into Maggie's porridge-splattered face.

"Mama said I could wait for you," declared Billy-the-Pain.

Penny sighed. Mrs. Hanson was just making sure that her precious Billy didn't go near the Fowlie house. They had the diphtheria. The two youngest died last week within days of each other, poor things.

Penny wet the tea, not that she'd have time for a mug, and did her best to ignore Billy-the-Beastly.

"Come on, Penny, let's go down to the docks," Billy whined.

"I will not. Anyway, who says that ships crashed into one another?" Penny spooned the last bit of porridge into Maggie's mouth, then wiped her face with a cloth. "Good girl. All gone."

"Must be true." Billy's voice rose to a high-pitched whine. "There's smoke reaching the sky." He grabbed hold of Penny's hand.

"Stop pulling." Penny shook Billy loose and followed him through the parlour and down the hallway.

"Look!" said Billy as he flung open the front door.

Penny stared out into the road. She could hardly believe her eyes! People were standing at windows craning to see down the road to the port, racing down the street to see the collision first-hand, or just standing, arms crossed, tsk-tsking about all them foreign boats running around, bound to crash into each other sooner or latter. Tsk-tsk.

Penny too craned her neck to see the port. A dark column of smoke, with lightning-quick flashes through it, rose up over the buildings. It was down at the harbour all right. Near the Narrows. Papa had his office down there; maybe he was watching the ships too.

"It's nothing to do with us, Billy." Penny tried

Penny craned her neck to see the
port. A dark column of smoke
rose up over the buildings. It was
down at the harbour all right.

to pull Billy-the-Brat back into the house, but he would have nothing to do with it. He twisted out of Penny's grasp just as the paperboy flew past on his bicycle tossing his newspapers every which way. Penny looked down at the the *Herald's* headline: "Germans Start New Offensive to Take Venice."

"Oh honestly, the war. Everything is about the war," Penny huffed.

It was called the Great War, although Penny couldn't see what was so great about it. Not with all the young men coming back on ships from Europe all bandaged up, some with legs and arms missing. Still, the people in Halifax had to make ready for an invasion from the Germans. Why would the Germans want to come to Halifax? Penny's teacher, Mr. Shirley, said that Halifax was a great port, the best natural harbour in the world. Huge convoys of ships gathered in Bedford Basin to make the voyage across the Atlantic. The Germans would like to blow up all the ships that sailed out of Halifax.

"I'm going to go see." Billy made for the gate.

"You'll do no such thing." Penny reached out for him a second time. Too late, he was off. As if his nine-year-old legs were wheels, he sped down the road towards the wharf to see what was what.

"Well!" Penny shook her head. Billy was not her problem, but truth be told, Penny would have liked to have been running right beside him. Maybe she could ...

"Penny!" Emily cried from the kitchen, "Maggie threw her porridge bowl on the floor and it's all broke!"

CHAPTER N° 3

"Too hot." Emily set to unbuttoning the buttons on her coat, which Penny had just buttoned.

"Don't," Penny snapped. "It might turn cold later on. And put on your hat and mittens."

Penny poured milk into Maggie's bottle and struggled to attach the dummy. If it wasn't on just right, it would fly off and Maggie would be covered with milk.

"There!" Penny gave the bottle a satisfied shake, wrapped it in a tea towel and tucked it into

Maggie's baby bag. The clock chimed nine. No time for so much as a sip of tea.

It was a chore getting Maggie into her leggings and wool coat.

"Stay still!" Penny tied the hat strings under Maggie's chin and nearly forced her little hands into her mitts. Maggie squirmed. "Outside, Emily. Wait for me in the front by the pram." Penny pulled on her old blue coat and did up the three big buttons. The fur collar that Mama had taken from her own coat brushed her face. The coat was too small, but how could she give up the last thing Mama had made for her? Maybe Mrs. Hanson could help her let it out a bit.

Penny jammed her lunch bag into her pocket alongside her mittens and wool hat, slung her book bag over one shoulder and Maggie's baby bag over the other, then heaved Maggie up on one hip. "Ohhh," she moaned and sagged under the weight.

Maggie arched her back and let out a wail.

"Oh Maggie, stop it!" Penny charged through

the house to the front door.

"Look!" Emily stood by the garden gate and pointed to the grey-black billowing smoke that continued to rise in the distance.

"I see it." Penny didn't so much as look in that direction. Instead, she tumbled Maggie onto an old quilt that lay in the bottom of the great pram and tucked it around her.

" 'Fire!' " Emily jumped up and clapped her hands. " 'Fire, fire,' said Mr. McGuire. 'Where, where?' said Mrs. O'Hare. 'Down the town,' said Mr. Brown." Emily clapped her mittened hands and danced as she sang her rhyme.

"Emily, enough!" Penny huffed. "Do you want to ride or walk?" The pram could fit both girls if they didn't wiggle too much. Besides, there was no time for Emily to dawdle. Mrs. Hanson may be only a few doors down, but Emily could turn a short walk into a day's journey.

"I want to go see the fire." Emily stomped about. "I want to see the fire! 'Fire, fire,' said Mr. McGuire. 'Where, where?' said Mrs. O'Hare."

"No! I have to get to school!" Bloomfield School wasn't far, but at this rate she'd be half an hour late.

Penny scooped up the wriggling Emily in her arms and sat her face to face with Maggie in the pram. Then came the explosion.

The ground pitched and buckled. It rolled as if a giant at the centre of the earth were turning over. Then came the thunder, bigger than thunder, like all the thundering from the beginning of time was rolled up into one mighty crash. And then, as if she were no more than a bit of paper, Penny was lifted up into the air, up and up, and just as suddenly slapped back onto the ground.

Seconds later came the smashing and breaking of glass and the splintering of wood. "Mama," Penny sobbed, and then, "Papa."

She lay flat out on the road, yards from where she had last stood. What was it? What had happened? Had the Germans come? Had the war come to Halifax?

"Maggie. Emily," she whispered.

Her arms and legs would not move, would not obey.

"My eyes," she heard, over and over. Not one voice but ten, a hundred. People calling out, "Help me, my eyes. I'm blind. Help me!"

Penny pulled her legs up and then pushed up on her arms. She rested for a moment on her hands and knees. Up, up. "Emily," she whispered. Time went by. How much?

A black rain began to fall. It was oily and choked her. Penny spat on the ground. There was screaming and the roar of fire and through it she heard whimpering, like the sounds of kittens caught in a trap.

"Maggie, I'm coming." She had to stand, but there was nothing to grab onto, nothing to pull herself up with.

Penny flipped over and thumped down on the hard, surprised ground. Her eyes began to focus. Through the black rain she looked up the street. Where was she? What was this place? Many houses sagged. Every house was windowless. People ran in every direction, their faces streaming with blood, shards of glass sticking out of their heads, their faces, their bodies. Some were naked, their clothes blown away by the explosion.

"Emily! Maggie!" Penny stood and the world seemed to shift. She blinked, tried to focus. *Walk,* she commanded her legs. *Walk.* Her house? Where was her house? There. It was tilted but still standing. The doors and windows had been blown in.

"Billy!" Mrs. Hanson, a big woman who never ran, came running. "Billy? Billy!"

She stopped in front of Penny. "Have you seen my Billy?" she cried.

Who was Billy? She couldn't think. She didn't answer but only stared up at the woman's blackened face.

Mrs. Hanson spun around and ran down the road, screaming her son's name. The next scream came from Penny as she sank to the ground. A piece of glass as big as a plate was sticking out of Mrs. Hanson's back.

CHAPTER N⁰ 4

Penny reached up and touched her head.
Blood poured down from a gash above her eyes.
She wiped her forehead with her sleeve and
cocked her head towards the sounds of whimpering. There! They were coming from the
overturned pram. It was wedged between a huge
piece of wood and the side of the house. Penny
stood on two trembling legs and blundered across
the road towards the pram. A crowd of shell-
shocked people were stumbling up from the
harbour. A slight, ten-year-old girl was no match

for the force of fearful people lurching and lumbering towards her. It was as if the road rose up and pulled her back down to the ground. And then something big crashed down on her legs. She scrambled back and pulled her legs to her chest. People were stepping on her! "Oh, oh, get away, away!" Penny flung her arms out in front of her face and batted at the air. "Away, away."

"Zeppelins," someone cried, "German Zeppelins."

"It's the end of the world," howled another. "Repent. It's the end of the world."

Hand over hand Penny crawled towards the pram. Again she stood and lurched forward. "Maggie, Emily, where are you? Please, please God, help me find my sisters. Please."

The pram's large underbelly faced the blackened sky. Its wheels, still attached, spun on their own.

A blown-out window frame pinned the pram firmly to the ground and the side of the house. Glass and bits of wood and debris covered everything.

"Emily? Maggie? Please, please be all right." Penny tried to lift the wooden frame. Bits of glass and splinters scored her hands. She dropped it. It was heavy, too heavy.

"Help!" she called out to the street. "Help me, my sisters are under here!" she yelled, and then she tried to lift it again.

"Stand back." A woman, her face hidden by a dark scarf, came up behind Penny.

"I can lift too." Penny lunged forward.

"Back!" the woman commanded, with such force that Penny obeyed.

"Please, please be all right," Penny whispered, her eyes fixed firmly on the upside-down pram.

With a mighty tug, the woman heaved, and then tossed the window frame aside, as if it were nothing, as if she were lifting feathers. As if she had the strength of an angel.

"Thank you, thank you," Penny sobbed. She bent down and, with bloody hands, gently lifted the shell of pram.

Four small, frightened eyes stared back at her. There they were, safe, like two kittens in a lair.

"Penny!" Emily threw herself in her sister's arms. "Bomb. Bomb."

"Yes, my love." Penny held Emily tight as she reached for Maggie. Maggie's eyes were wide with fright but she wasn't crying. Not a sound escaped her lips.

"Put on your gloves," said the woman, "and your hat. They're in your pocket."

"Yes, yes." Penny searched through her pockets and did as she was told. "Thank you." Wait. How did she know that her gloves were in her pocket? Penny turned to look up at the woman. Where did she go? The woman had vanished, as if she had never been there at all!

"Bomb, bomb," Emily cried.

"Oh, Emily." Penny turned her attention back to her sisters and held both girls as tightly as she could.

"I'm sorry that I was cross with you this morning. I'll never be cross with you again. Never." Penny buried her face in Emily's coat. "Maggie." Penny pulled the baby in tight. "It wasn't your fault that Mama died. It wasn't. I didn't mean to blame you. I love you." Penny sobbed as though her heart would break.

Baby Maggie let herself be hugged but did nothing to return it. She didn't blink, not even baby sounds escaped her lips.

A sharp crack sounded. Penny's head snapped back. It was ominous and there was no mistaking it, it came from the house. A beam had broken. She looked up. The house would fall on top of them if they didn't move quickly. Penny scrambled to her feet and turned the pram over. It rocked back and forth for a moment before settling.

A green, horse-drawn, two-wheeled cart, with the word COAL printed on the side, came roaring up the road. "Run," yelled the driver, "there's more to blow. The barracks," he cried. "The fire has reached the Wellington Barracks!" He cracked his whip, and the horse, its eyes wide with fright, reared, then stumbled onward through the debris.

"There are explosives in there," Penny cried. "We have to get out of here. Hurry! Come on, both of you."

With a strength Penny didn't know she had, she hoisted both girls up at once, tossed them into the pram and buried them under the quilt. The baby bag landed on top. Penny turned the pram to face the street.

The crowd on the road moved like a mass. They were heading towards Citadel Hill, the great British fortress that dominated Halifax. How would she get this pram up the hill? The wheels were loppy to begin with and now each one seemed to go in a different direction. With all the strength she could muster, Penny pushed the pram into the crowd and joined the stream of humanity that was charging up the hill.

CHAPTER N.º 5

The next few hours passed in a blur. Penny pushed the pram over broken cobblestones, around uprooted trees and telephone poles that had been snapped in half, past churches and schools that had been hollowed out like sand castles. Dangling live wires, swinging freely, crackled and sparked in the air. Fires, some engulfing entire houses, others smouldering, burned on every side. Penny didn't look back. *Don't look back.*

It was cold, freezing cold. Still, sweat poured down her face. Penny pushed and shoved the pram through the hordes of people that moved at a lumbering pace. Bleeding, broken men, women and children stumbled about. Some were being carried on makeshift litters, some in wheelbarrows. She passed soldiers, destined for the front, hauling the wounded across their backs, as though they were already in the trenches. She passed dead people. And Papa, she tried not to think of Papa.

There was talk. "Fifty German U-boats are in the harbour."

Another voice shrieked, "The entire German fleet has landed. It's the invasion of Canada!"

"Papa, please, help us. Papa, please." Penny prayed and pushed, prayed and pushed.

"Make way," hollered a man standing on the

running board of an automobile edging its way through the moving crowd. "Make way, ambulance coming through." It wasn't an ambulance, not a real one, but an auto filled with wounded people. It passed so close to Penny that, had the window been down, she could have reached in and touched the driver. And then she recognized him.

"Uncle Robert!" Penny shouted. "Robert!" It was him. It was him! It was Aunt Colleen's brother. "Help!" Penny thumped the window. "It's me, Penny." She let go of the pram's handles and, with both fists now, hammered the side of the auto as it passed. "It's me, Penny. It's me. Stop!" But Robert didn't hear, couldn't hear through the cries and sobs of those around him.

The car inched forward through the crowds. As it moved past, people filled its wake. And then it was gone. Swallowed up.

"Penny!" Emily screamed from inside the pram. "Penny!"

The pram!

"Emmmm!" Penny spun around. The pram was

rolling backwards, back down the hill! It became caught in the surging crowd. It twisted and turned around. It rocked with a fury, back and forth.

"No! No!" Penny shrieked as she ran, shoving and pushing. "My sisters! My sisters!" She swung her arms, any way, all ways, hitting anyone. "Let me through." She fell into the path of a wheelbarrow and felt its front wheel ram into her stomach. Penny pulled her legs up and twisted out of its path. The man pushing the wheelbarrow didn't stop, couldn't stop. His two small children lay curled up in the bottom, asleep.

Up again, the pain in her stomach making her stumble in all directions. Where was it? Where did it go? There! Penny ran. The pram had come to rest against a fallen tree.

"Maggie!" Penny ripped back the top of the pram and stared inside. Emily cried out; Maggie, unblinking, just stared ahead.

"Hush, hush," Penny whispered as she bent down and gathered them to her. "Hush, don't cry. We are all right."

Penny looked up. They'd lost ground. Grabbing the handle of the pram, she gave it a mighty shove and once again, started up the hill.

The slopes of Citadel Hill were littered with ragged, damaged, broken people. The crowd grew thicker as she tried to get closer to the walls of the old fortress. They would have to leave the pram behind.

"Emily—" Penny stopped "—you'll have to walk now."

Emily whimpered and snuggled closer to her baby sister.

"Come on, you can do it." Penny scooped Emily out of the pram and set her down on her two wobbly legs. She immediately sank to the ground.

"Come on, you are a big girl. You can do it."

Penny reached back into the pram and pulled out the baby bag. Like a small miracle, the baby bottle inside was unbroken. She flung the bag over her head so that it hung down her back.

"Up you get, Emily. Stand up, you can do it." Emily struggled to stand on her five-year-old legs as Penny reached in and hoisted Maggie into her arms.

The pain in her stomach shot up and Penny staggered under the weight of the one-year-old.

With one arm around Maggie, Penny reached back into the pram, grabbed the quilt and flung it over the baby.

The walls of the Citadel were not far; still, it seemed like miles. Penny stumbled onward, the baby clutching her, Emily holding on to her coattails. "See? We're going up there, beside the wall. Come on." They picked their way through the ash-covered faces. Some huddled together, others sat silently. She could hear bits of prayers, most uttered quietly, some sung to the heavens.

"*Our Father, Who art in Heaven…*"

"*But he that trusteth in the Lord, mercy shall compass him about.*"

And from a clutch of people huddled around a few smouldering sticks, "*in nomine patris, et filii, et spiritus sancti,*" in the name of the Father, and the Son, and of the Holy Ghost.

Grey people wrapped in rags huddled together, warming themselves around a small fire. At last they found a spot against the Citadel wall. Penny spread the quilt out as best she could, sat Maggie and Emily down side by side and tucked the quilt around them.

"Here, Maggie." Penny pulled the baby bottle out of the bag and passed it to her sister. Maggie shoved it in her mouth and sucked. It was then that Penny realized that Maggie hadn't cried, hadn't made a sound since the explosion. "Emily, eat this." Penny plunged her hand into her coat pocket and took out a flattened sandwich. Emily shook her head furiously and then buried herself under the quilt. Well, maybe it was better to save the food they had. Who knew how long they would have to wait for their next meal? Penny shoved the sandwich back into her pocket.

She was so cold. They were all cold. Her fingers and toes were numb. Scrunching and unscrunching them did no good. Penny leaned against the Citadel wall and looked towards the harbour. Boats scooted madly from one place to another looking for survivors that had fallen off ships or been washed into the water. The South End of Halifax looked safe enough, but from this distance she couldn't see the blown-out windows or the havoc. Then Penny turned her face to the North End. It was now a sea of flames and belching black smoke.

Penny covered her blackened face with her blood-crusted hands. "Papa, our home," she cried, her body heaving with sobs, "and my blue dress."

Grey people wrapped in rags
huddled together, warming
themselves around a small fire. At
last they found a spot near the
Citadel wall.

CHAPTER N° 6

The weather was changing. There was something in the air, a storm maybe. Penny, Maggie and Emily huddled together. Penny could hardly whisper through her chattering teeth and blue, cracked lips.

"Here you go, children." Penny's head snapped up and she stared at a woman who, basket in hand, was giving out packets of biscuits.

"Thank you," Penny whispered. She passed the biscuits to Emily.

Emily screeched.

"What is it? What's wrong?"

Penny looked into Emily's open palm. The biscuits were covered in blood. "Hush, Emily," Penny whispered into her sister's ear. "Hush now. It's just blood. Look, I'll throw it away." Penny took a biscuit from Emily's hand and pitched it down the hill. "See, all gone."

"I'm cold." Emily nibbled at the biscuit.

"I know." Penny wrapped her arms around Emily and pulled her close. "I know."

"All clear!" Soldiers bellowed into mega-phones. "All clear." There would be no more explosions. They could go back to their homes now.

"Where are the Germans?" someone shouted.

"What about the invasion?"

The crowd demanded answers.

There were no Germans and there was no invasion. Two ships, one loaded with explosives for the war in Europe, the other bound for New York, had collided. One of them blew up. It was a soldier who said all this in a matter-of-fact voice, but then, he was back from the war and nothing could surprise him now.

"How many?" gasped a woman. "How many dead?"

"Hard to tell," shrugged the soldier, and he began to bellow into his megaphone once again.

Penny scrambled to her feet, skirted a small fire and the people huddled around it, and grabbed hold of the soldier's sleeve.

"My father, he was down at the dock." Penny's voice broke.

"Nothing left standing down there. Wouldn't hold out much hope, miss," the soldier said briskly as he limped away.

Penny carefully picked her way back to her sisters.

A thought, one that had been nibbling at the edge of her mind, now hit her with such force that she crumpled forward.

Papa was dead.

"Come on. We have to go." Penny scooped up Maggie.

"Where?" Emily sobbed. "Where are we going? Penny, where?"

"Home," Penny replied.

With baby Maggie in her arms and Emily clutching her coattail, Penny staggered back down the hill towards Macara Street. The sight of the streets below took Penny's breath away. It was as if a hand of steel had come down and hammered her whole world.

"Don't look, Emily," Penny cried. "Just hold on to me." Penny pressed Maggie's head against her fur collar and hoped the baby was asleep, but Maggie's eyes were wide open, taking in everything.

Penny, too, tried not to look at the lacerated faces, the lost souls staggering around her. And then they were home, or what was left of it. Only the back wall of the house remained standing.

"Gone," Emily cried, "all gone."

Penny sat Emily against the wall and settled Maggie beside her, then tiptoed though the cinder and ash, broken boards, smashed bricks. There were bits of things she recognized, the handle of a cup, hinges from the cupboard, half a book. The clock! Mama's clock! There it was on the floor, its face smashed. Penny seized it.

"What should I do?"

Staggering back to her sisters, Penny huddled beside them and closed her eyes.

"Penny!" The voice was far away, as if in a dream. Penny drifted in and out of sleep. She was back in her own bed, with Maggie tucked in beside her. She was warm. Warm.

"Penny!"

The voice held such urgency, such pain.

"Penny!"

It was fading now. Going farther and farther away. Her eyes flew open.

Papa! Where was he? Was it him? Had she dreamed it?

"Papa!" Penny struggled to her feet.

"Penny, don't go." Emily, too, awoke.

"Stay here, Emily, stay with Maggie," Penny hollered as she ran, ran after the voice, around the wall and into what was once their street.

"Papa," she wailed. Where was he?

"PAPA!" He wasn't there. "PAPA!"

A ragged man with a face like a coal miner, his clothes a bloody mess and all but torn off him, looked back. His arms had turned blue with the cold. Was it him?

"Papa?"

The man stopped, looked, and then staggered towards her, his arms outstretched long before he reached her. And then he was holding her, his face buried in her hair.

"My girl," he sobbed. "My beautiful Irish girl."

He held her so tightly that the warmth of him spread over her like a blanket. "I thought," he sputtered and stopped. "Your head? Are you hurt?"

Penny felt herself lifted up into the air and carried in his arms as if she were nothing more than a piece of cloud.

"No, no, I'm fine. Oh, Papa." Penny held on to him, tight, tighter.

Papa pulled away. Fear suddenly filled his eyes. "Your sisters?"

"They're fine too, Papa. Look, over there, behind the wall."

Penny felt herself lifted up into the air and carried in his arms as if she were nothing more than a piece of cloud. He fell on his knees in front of his girls and scooped them up, kissing each one. Kissing and hugging. "Thank you." He threw his head back and cried to the open sky. "Thank you."

Emily's tears flowed and mixed with Penny's and Papa's. Only little Maggie remained unmoved, her unblinking eyes just staring up at Papa's blackened face.

"Look." Emily pulled out Mama's broken clock and handed it to Papa. "Penny found it!"

There was nothing more that could surprise him this day. He took it in hand and laughed, laughed long and loud.

"All broken," said Emily.

"It can be fixed, Emily." Tears slid down Papa's face.

"Papa, a soldier said that down by the harbour everyone was killed." Penny struggled to speak through her own tears and chattering teeth.

"I was out on a job, my darlin'. Safe enough. I've been back here three times searching for you. Oh, my lovely girls. Come on. Shelters are set up around the city. You need to get warm."

"Billy Hanson, Papa, he went down to the harbour . . ." Penny's voice trailed off.

"I haven't seen him, but don't give up hope. Come now." He heaved Maggie and Emily up into his arms.

"What will we do without a house?"

"We'll build a new one, a fine one fit for my angels." Again Papa looked up to the sky, as though he were talking to someone else.

"Does that mean that I won't have to go to Montreal to live?" Penny's words came out in such a rush that she was left breathless with the effort.

"We'll stay together and make do with what the Lord has given us."

"Oh, Papa." Penny leaned against him.

Papa kissed the tops of Emily's and Maggie's heads over and over as he walked, as if he couldn't get enough of them, as if he couldn't believe his blessings. He looked down at Penny, and there was nothing but love in his eyes. "Your mama would be proud of what you have done this day."

ENDNOTE

On December 6, 1917, two ships collided in the narrowest part of Halifax Harbour. One ship, called the Imo, was heading for New York. The other ship, the Mont Blanc, was loaded with a huge stock of highly explosive materials destined for the war.

Of the more than 65,000 people who lived in Halifax, over 1,900 were killed, although no completely accurate statistics are available. Flying glass blinded 37 people while another 250 eyes had to be removed. Over two and a half kilometres of land around the harbour was completely destroyed. Then fires sprang up. And, as if this weren't enough, the next day a terrible snowstorm blanketed the city. Among the devastation and ruins, Penny and her sisters and thousands of others fought for their lives.

Acknowledgements

Cindy Kantor, who brought the idea for

the series to Penguin.

Barbara Berson, senior editor.

Catherine Marjoribanks, copy editor.

Janet Kitz, writer, historian and brilliant fact checker.

Shannon Proulx, production editor,

patient in the extreme.

D. J. (Ian) McKay, father and fastidious editor.

Katie Parsons, intrepid reader.

Thanks also to Mrs. Aileen Meagher for passing along

her story of the biscuits as retold on page 55.

Dear Reader,

Did you enjoy reading this Our Canadian Girl adventure? Write us and tell us what you think! We'd love to hear about your favourite parts, which characters you like best, and even whom else you'd like to see stories about. Maybe you'd like to read an adventure with one of Our Canadian Girls that happened in your hometown—fifty, a hundred years ago or more!

Send your letters to:

Our Canadian Girl

c/o Penguin Canada

10 Alcorn Avenue, Suite 300

Toronto, ON M4V 3B2

Be sure to check your bookstore for more books in the Our Canadian Girl series. There are some ready for you right now, and more are on their way.

We look forward to hearing from you!

Sincerely,

Barbara Berson

PENGUIN BOOKS CANADA

P.S. Don't forget to visit us online at www.ourcanadiangirl.ca—there are some other girls you should meet!

Canada's

1608
Samuel de
Champlain
establishes
the first
fortified
trading post
at Quebec.

1759
The British
defeat the
French in
the Battle
of the
Plains of
Abraham.

1812
The United
States
declares war
against
Canada.

1845
The expedition of
Sir John Franklin
to the Arctic ends
when the ship is
frozen in the pack
ice; the fate of its
crew remains a
mystery.

1869
Louis Riel
leads his
Métis
followers in
the Red
River
Rebellion.

1871
British
Columbia
joins
Canada.

1755
The British
expel the
entire French
population
of Acadia
(today's
Maritime
provinces),
sending
them into
exile.

1776
The 13
Colonies
revolt
against
Britain, and
the Loyalists
flee to
Canada.

1837
Calling for
responsible
government, the
Patriotes, following
Louis-Joseph
Papineau, rebel in
Lower Canada;
William Lyon
Mackenzie leads the
uprising in Upper
Canada.

1867
New
Brunswick,
Nova Scotia
and the United
Province of
Canada come
together in
Confederation
to form the
Dominion of
Canada.

1870
Manitoba joins
Canada. The
Northwest
Territories
become an
official
territory of
Canada.

1783
Rachel

Timeline

1885
At Craigellachie, British Columbia, the last spike is driven to complete the building of the Canadian Pacific Railway.

1898
The Yukon Territory becomes an official territory of Canada.

1914
Britain declares war on Germany, and Canada, because of its ties to Britain, is at war too.

1918
As a result of the Wartime Elections Act, the women of Canada are given the right to vote in federal elections.

1945
World War II ends conclusively with the dropping of atomic bombs on Hiroshima and Nagasaki.

1873
Prince Edward Island joins Canada.

1896
Gold is discovered on Bonanza Creek, a tributary of the Klondike River.

1905
Alberta and Saskatchewan join Canada.

1917
In the Halifax harbour, two ships collide, causing an explosion that leaves more than 1,600 dead and 9,000 injured.

1939
Canada declares war on Germany seven days after war is declared by Britain and France.

1949
Newfoundland, under the leadership of Joey Smallwood, joins Canada.

1896
Emily

1885
Marie-Claire

1917
Penelope

Don't miss your chance to meet all the girls in the Our Canadian Girl series...

The story takes place in Montreal, during the smallpox epidemic of 1885. Marie-Claire, who lives in a humble home with her working-class family, must struggle to persevere through the illness of her cousin Lucille and the work-related injury of her father – even to endure the death of a loved one. All the while, Marie-Claire holds out hope for the future.

It's 1896 and Emily lives a middle-class life in Victoria, B.C., with her parents and two little sisters. She becomes friends with Hing, the family's Chinese servant and, through that relationship, discovers the secret world of Victoria's Chinatown.

Ten-year-old Rachel arrives in northern Nova Scotia in 1783 with her mother, where they reunite with Rachel's stepfather after escaping slavery in South Carolina. Their joy at gaining freedom in a safe new home is dashed when they arrive, for the land they are given is barren and they don't have enough to eat. How will they survive?

Watch for more Canadian girls in 2002...

Penguin Books Canada Ltd. • www.ourcanadiangirl.ca